The Bear, the Piano, the Dog and the Fiddle

For Katie, Ben and George
—D.L.

Brimming with creative inspiration, how-to projects, and useful information to enrich your everyday life, Quarto Knows is a favourite destination for those pursuing their interests and passions. Visit our site and dig deeper with our books into your area of interest: Quarto Creates, Quarto Cooks, Quarto Homes, Quarto Lives, Quarto Drives, Quarto Explores, Quarto Gifts, or Quarto Kids.

First published in 2018 by Lincoln Children's Books, an imprint of The Quarto Group.
First paperback edition first published in 2019 by Lincoln Children's Books, an imprint of
The Quarto Group,
The Old Brewery, 6 Blundell Street, London N7 9BH, United Kingdom.
T (0)20 7700 6700 F (0)20 7700 8066
www.QuartoKnows.com
The right of David Litchfield to be identified as the author of this work has been asserted by him in accordance with the Copyright, Designs and Patents Act, 1988 (United Kingdom).

ISBN 978-1-78603-595-0

The illustrations were created digitally
Set in Granjon LT
Published by Rachel Williams
Designed by Andrew Watson
Edited by Katie Cotton
Production by Kate O'Riordan and Jenny Cundill

Manufactured in Guangdong, China TT112018

1 3 5 7 9 8 6 4 2

The Bear, the Piano, the Dog and the Fiddle

David Litchfield

LINCOLN
Children's Books

Hector and Hugo were best friends. Hector was a fiddle player, and Hugo was one of his biggest fans.

Over the years, they'd had good times, bad times and even some crazy times.

But now, times weren't so great.
"What are we going to do, Hugo?" Hector said as they
walked home. "My act is yesterday's news. Who'd want
to listen to an old fiddler like me, when they can
watch a world-famous piano-playing bear?"

Hugo woofed to say that *he* would,
but Hector just sighed.

"I'm too old for this game, boy," he said, "I guess I'll never
get to play at the big concert hall, like I dreamed."

And with that, Hector packed away his fiddle forever.

Now that Hector didn't go out to play his fiddle,
he spent most of his time watching TV…

listening to music,

sleeping,

sleeping

and sleeping some more.

Hector and Hugo's neighbourhood was
noisy, so Hector kept the windows shut
when he slept. But one night, he forgot.

In the early hours of the morning,
a strange noise woke him up.

Hector
crept out
of bed,

tiptoed
up the
corridor,

and pushed
open the
door to
the roof.

Hugo was playing Hector's fiddle,
and the music Hugo was making was
toe-tappingly,
finger-clickingly,
whistle-blowingly
AWESOME!

Hector's tummy hurt a bit when he saw everyone in the neighbourhood nodding along, but then he saw something else... how much his friend LOVED to play.

The next morning, Hector taught Hugo all the
tricks of the trade he'd learnt over the years.

Before long, a crowd had gathered
to hear the toe-tapping tunes.

News of the incredible fiddle-playing dog spread,
and one day, a very famous bear came to watch.

Bear told Hugo that he was starting a band full of musical animals. He invited him to come on tour and play his fiddle to hundreds of thousands of people.

As Hugo looked up at Hector, his tail wagging, Hector's tummy started to hurt again. "I guess you should go," he said, trying to smile. "It's the opportunity of a lifetime."

Hugo's tail wagged even more as he packed to go away with Bear's Big Band, making sure the fiddle was safely stowed away.

But Hector began to have second thoughts. "Don't go and join that silly group, Hugo," he said. "We don't need them."

Hugo put his head on Hector's knee,
but Hector pushed him away.

"Fine," said Hector. "I'm sure you'll be back with your
tail between your legs. You're not even that good!"

Hugo picked up his suitcase and left.
Suddenly, Hector felt awful. "WAIT, Hugo," he cried.
"I'm sor—"

But it was too late.

With Bear's Big Band, Hugo toured the world, playing spectacular shows to sold-out crowds of adoring fans.

Hugo was the star of the show,

with Bear on the piano, 'Big G' on drums,

and Clint 'The Wolfman' Jones grooving on the double bass.

Millions of people watched them all over the world
on their televisions and computer screens…

Millions of people including Hector.
As he watched, Hector missed making music.
He missed playing his fiddle.

But most of all, he missed his friend.

TONIGHT: BEAR'S B

Months passed, until one day when Hector saw
some posters saying that Bear's Big Band were
playing at the big concert hall in their city.

Hector wanted to go, but then he
remembered the horrible thing he had said.

What if Hugo didn't want him there?

Hector bought a ticket anyway and found a spot at the front, right by the stage. He noticed that Hugo had a new fiddle, and wondered what had happened to his old one. But then the band started playing.

Hector couldn't believe how mind-blowingly, toe-tappingly, finger-clickingly
AWESOME the music was!

"Hugo!" he shouted. "It's me, Hector. You're brilliant! I'm so proud of you."

But Hugo just whispered something to the bear, who whispered something to a security guard, then they carried on playing.

A few minutes later, Hector felt two big paws grab him.

"What's going on?" he asked nervously.

The security guards picked up Hector and
took him into a dark corridor.

"It's OK," Hector said,
"I was going to leave anyway. LET ME GO!"
But the guards just kept walking with Hector squished
between them, until suddenly they stopped.

And Hector realized just where he was.

"Ladies and gentlemen," boomed a voice, "I'm pleased to announce that tonight Bear's Big Band will be joined by a VERY special guest."

"Please give a big welcome to Hector. I'm told that our star Hugo wouldn't be here without him."

As the crowd cheered, Hugo passed Hector his old fiddle, which he'd kept safe for all this time.
He woofed and wagged his tail.

And as Hector took the fiddle, he realized that though he and Hugo might have good times, bad times and even times apart, they would always be friends.

Because good friendship,
just like good music, lasts a lifetime.

David Litchfield first began drawing when he was very young. His illustration heroes and biggest influences are Albert Uderzo, Sylvain Chomet, Jon Klassen and Shaun Tan. He creates his unique, atmospheric artwork using a variety of traditional techniques, assembling the different elements together in Photoshop to create large-scale, dramatic scenes. *The Bear and the Piano*, David's first picture book, won the Waterstones' Children's Book Prize 2016, Illustrated Book Category, and became an international bestseller.